I AM READING
RICKY'S RAT GANG

ANTHONY MASTERS

Illustrated by

CHRIS FISHER

KINGFISH

D0258233

WORCESTERSHIRE COUNTY COUNCIL	
051	
Peters	25-Feb-2009
	£5.99

For my daughter's very dear friends
Jacob and Isaac Pursglove – A.M.
For Joe and Will – C.F.

KINGFISHER
An imprint of Kingfisher Publications Plc
New Penderel House, 283-288 High Holborn
London WC1V 7HZ
www.kingfisherpub.com

First published by Kingfisher 2002
This edition published 2007
2 4 6 8 10 9 7 5 3

Text copyright © Anthony Masters 2002
Illustrations copyright © Chris Fisher 2002

The moral right of the author and illustrator has been asserted.

All rights reserved. No part of this publication may be
reproduced, stored in a retrieval system or transmitted by
any means electronic, mechanical, photocopying or otherwise,
without the prior permission of the publisher.

A CIP catalogue record for this book is available from the British Library.

ISBN 978 0 7534 1487 3

Printed in China
2TR/0607/WKT/(CG)/115MA/C

Contents

Chapter One
Sugar Mountain

"We're going to have a treat,"
said Mel Mouse to his best friend,
Max. "Look!"
Someone had spilt a load
of sugar on the storeroom
floor.

The sugar looked like a
big white mountain.
"You stand guard.
I'll get Molly,"
said Max.

Max ran out into the supermarket.

It was late at night.

During the day the shop was

dangerous for mice.

There were people

pushing trolleys,

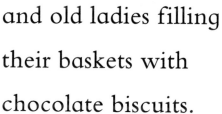

children playing

games,

and old ladies filling

their baskets with

chocolate biscuits.

But at night it was
even worse.

A security guard and his
dog kept watch in the shop.

The mice felt safer in the storeroom.

But Max knew Molly was in the shop.

He ran to the fruit section.

Molly was nibbling an apple.

"We've got a treat," said Max, grinning.

"Come and see."

The three mice gazed
up at the sugar mountain.
"We'll scoff the lot!" said
Molly. She was always hungry.
"We'll eat till we're sick!"
squeaked Mel.

Then suddenly a voice snarled,
"Get your dirty paws off that sugar.
It's ours."

Max was the first
to turn round.
He didn't like
what he saw.

Then Mel and Molly turned round.
They didn't like what they saw either.

Ricky Rat and his brother,

Ronnie, had squeezed under

the door of the storeroom.

Ricky's gang was close behind.

The rats wore dark glasses.

The rats were gangsters.

They often raided the supermarket

at night.

Too often.

Ricky Rat held up a great big

water balloon.

"Back off the sugar," he said.

"Or I'll squirt you silly!"

"It's not fair," said Molly Mouse,

her paws in the air. "It's mice only

in this storeroom. We got here first."

"There isn't room for rats *and* mice in
this supermarket," said Ricky.

"We're taking over," said Ronnie.

"This is *our* storeroom now."

Ricky threw the water balloon.

SPLAT!

Squeaking with fury, Mel, Max and
Molly ran away into the shop.

"We'll get you for this!" yelled Max.

But the rats weren't listening.

They were eating the sugar.

Chapter Two
Rat Attack

The mice ran across the floor of the
supermarket.

They were on the lookout for danger.

They were scared of the rats and
their big water balloons.

But they were also scared of the
security guard and his dog, Toby.

The mice hid behind a pot of flowers.
"Those rats are not getting away
with this," squeaked Mel.
"Soon there'll be no sugar left,"
wailed Molly.
"I've got a plan . . ." began Max.
Then suddenly he saw a long tail.
"Shhh – I think there's a rat
spying on us."

£1·99

Ronnie came out from behind the flowers. "Ricky says I've got to check on you," he said, with a sugary grin. "If you try anything, you'll get your tails nipped off."

Now the mice were really scared.
The rats were fierce. The mice had
had battles with them before –
and they'd lost them all.

But it wasn't fair! The mice had found
the storeroom first, so it belonged to
them. It was their hiding-place.
They *must* get rid of the rat gang.

Suddenly Toby the guard dog
ran out of the office.
The guard came too.
"Mice!" he yelled.
"Get them, Toby!"

The mice fled behind some cereal boxes.

Barking loudly, Toby charged.

Mel put his paws over his eyes.

So did Molly.

Max held his breath.

Then the telephone began to ring.

The guard ran back to his office . . .

and Toby ran with him.

The mice sighed with relief.

"Phew!" said Max. "That was close!"

Suddenly a jet of water
splashed down on them.
SPLAT!

"And I'm even
closer!" sneered
Ronnie Rat from
the top of a box
of cornflakes.
"So watch it!"

21

The mice were soaked.

"It's hopeless!" said Molly,

shivering. "We'll be stuck out

here forever."

"Toby will catch us if we can't get

back to the storeroom!"

wailed Mel.

"I've got a plan," said Max, and

he began to whisper . . .

Chapter Three
Rat Trap

Max, Mel and Molly ran to the pet
food section.

They found a bag of dry dog food.

The mice looked around carefully –
but there was no sign of Ronnie,
the guard or Toby.

With their sharp teeth the mice
made holes in the bag.
The dog food began to spill out.
The mice looked around again.
Everywhere was quiet.
"Now we need some paper cups,"
whispered Max.

Mel and Molly soon found a packet.
They dragged it back to Max.
"This is hard work," said Mel.
"Stop talking and hurry up,"
hissed Max. He was
getting worried.
At any moment the
guard and Toby
might come
out of the
office.

The mice filled some cups with dry dog food and carried them carefully to the storeroom door. Then they began to scatter the food in a trail towards the guard's office.

"I can't keep this up," complained Mel.

"Just get on with it," snapped Max. "If we don't hurry there'll be no sugar left."

"If that dog comes out," said Molly, "there'll be nothing of us left either."

At last the trail of dog food

led right up to the office door.

The door was open.

Toby was asleep in his basket.

"We'll have to wake Toby up," said

Max. "Then when he runs out of the

office he'll eat the dog food and

follow the trail . . ."

". . . right to the storeroom,"

finished Mel happily.

He wasn't tired any longer.

28

"Then he'll smell a rat – or two," said Molly, grinning.
"He'll smell us if we're not careful," said Max. "You two go and hide behind those tins of baked beans. I'll wake Toby up."

"We can't leave you," said Molly
bravely.

But Mel was a bit of a coward.

"Yes, we can," he said – and

ran off as fast as he could.

Chapter Four
The Guard Dog

In the storeroom, the rats were
still guzzling the sugar.

"Those mice have gone very quiet,"
said Ricky, wiping sugar off his
dark glasses. "What's happened
to them?"

Ronnie peered under the door.

"No mice in sight. But someone's
dropped something on the floor.
Maybe it's more sugar," said
Ronnie greedily.
"We haven't finished this lot yet!"
said Ricky.

Bravely, Max Mouse crept into the
guard's office.

He squeaked loudly into Toby's ear –

and ran.

Toby smelt mouse and bounded after him.
Now he smelt dog food too.

Max joined Molly and Mel behind the
tins of beans. The three mice watched
Toby anxiously.

Toby began to eat the dog food.

He ate all the way to the storeroom door.

Then he began to bark.

Inside, the rat gang stopped eating.

"We're trapped," said Ronnie.

"It's those dirty mice," snapped Ricky,
pulling his hat right down to his
glasses.

"Mice who bark?" asked Ronnie.

"That's a dog, you fool!" said Ricky.

"Those mice must have set us up."

"So now there's no way out!" cried

Ronnie.

"But there's a way in," hissed
Ricky.

He dived into the sugar mountain.

Ronnie and the rest of the gang
followed him.

Chapter Five
Mice Rule

The guard pushed open the storeroom
door.

Toby dashed in, growling and barking.

The rats burrowed even deeper into the
sugar.

But their tails were still sticking out.

"Rats!" shouted the guard. "Rats in the storeroom! Get them, Toby!"

"Let's get out of here!" yelled Ricky, pulling himself out of the sugar mountain.

Ronnie and the gang were close behind him.

They dived between Toby's legs,
and out through the open door.
Toby chased after them.

41

The rats ran past the shelf where the
mice were hiding.

"You're finished," the mice squeaked.

"We rule the storeroom now."

The rats escaped through a hole under the back door of the supermarket.

"We'll be back!" yelled Ricky, as he and the gang scuttled away into the night.

The guard and Toby went back
to the office and the door
slammed shut.

The mice jumped off the shelf
and ran to the storeroom.

There was no guard, no dog and
no rat gang to stop them now.

There was plenty of the sugar
mountain left.

As they began to eat, Molly said,
"You know what? Those rats will
be back. They won't give up."

"But now we've beaten them once, we can beat them again!" said Max.

"You bet we will," said Mel. He was feeling braver now. "Those rats are cowards. This is *our* storeroom."

"And we won't let them forget it!" said Molly.

"No," said Max. "Mice rule forever!"

About the Author and Illustrator

Anthony Masters used to run a children's theatre, and also held drama and writing courses in schools and libraries. But he is best known for his own stories for children. He said, "I've often imagined what it might be like in a supermarket when it is closed at night. I think it would be a bit scary in the dark!"

Chris Fisher's favourite subject at school was art, and now he is the illustrator of more than 60 books for children. He loved drawing all the characters in the story and imagining their adventures in the supermarket. He says, "I wonder if there are any mice in my local supermarket – and whether they are as brave as Max and his friends!"

Tips for Beginner Readers

1. Think about the cover and the title of the book. What do you think it will be about? While you are reading, think about what might happen next and why.

2. As you read, ask yourself if what you're reading makes sense. If it doesn't, try rereading or look at the pictures for clues.

3. If there is a word that you do not know, look carefully at the letters, sounds and word parts that you do know. Blend the sounds to read the word. Is this a word you know? Does it make sense in the sentence?

4. Think about the characters, where the story takes place, and the problems the characters in the story faced. What are the important ideas in the beginning, middle and end of the story?

5. Ask yourself questions like:
Did you like the story?
Why or why not?
How did the author make it fun to read?
How well did you understand it?

Maybe you can understand the story better if you read it again!